by Mike Thaler
IN THE MIDDLE OF THE PUDDLE
pictures by Bruce Degen

Harper & Row, Publishers

In the Middle of the Puddle

Text copyright © 1988 by Mike Thaler
Illustrations copyright © 1988 by Bruce Degen
Printed in the U.S.A. All rights reserved.
Typography by Bettina Rossner
1   2   3   4   5   6   7   8   9   10
First Edition

Library of Congress Cataloging-in-Publication Data
Thaler, Mike, date
    In the middle of the puddle.

    Summary: A frog and a turtle watch the rain turn
their puddle into an ocean before the sun comes along
and returns things to normal.
    [1. Frogs—Fiction.   2. Turtles—Fiction.
3. Rain and rainfall—Fiction]   I. Degen, Bruce, ill.
II. Title.
PZ7.T3In 1988   [E]   85-45830
ISBN 0-06-026053-X
ISBN 0-06-026054-8 (lib. bdg.)

For Lila who first told it
and Sara who first heard it
M.T.

For Miriam and Steve
B.D.

Once upon a time
a frog named Fred
and a turtle named Ted
lived in a puddle.
It was a little puddle
just big enough
for the two of them.

Every day
they sat
and looked at
the grass,
the flowers,
and the trees.
"I love our puddle," said Fred.

And every night
they sat
and watched
the fireflies,
the stars,
and the moon.
"I love our puddle too," said Ted.

8

Then one day
a giant cloud
came over their puddle.
It grumbled and rained on them!
And their puddle
got bigger,
turning into...

11

a pool.
And in the middle
of the pool
sat a frog named Fred
and a turtle named Ted.
But it didn't stop raining.
It rained,
and the pool
got bigger,
turning into...

a pond.
And in the middle
of the pond
sat a frog named Fred
and a turtle named Ted.
But it didn't stop raining.
It rained,
and it rained,
and the pond
got bigger,
and bigger,
turning into. . .

a lake.
And in the middle
of the lake
sat a frog named Fred
and a turtle named Ted.
But it didn't stop raining.
It rained,
and it rained,
and it rained,
and the lake got bigger,
and bigger,
and bigger,
turning into...

a sea!
And in the middle
of the sea
sat a frog named Fred
and a turtle named Ted.
And all they could see
was water.

"I wish it would stop raining,"
said Fred.
"So do I," said Ted.

Just then
the sun rolled by
and bumped that giant gray cloud
right out of the sky.

Now the sun
was all over them,
bright and warm.
It shined,
and it shined.
And the sea
got smaller,
and smaller,
and turned into...

a lake.
And the sun
kept shining
until the lake
got smaller,
and smaller,
and turned into. . .

a pond.
And the sun
kept on shining
until the pond
turned into. . .

a pool.
And the sun did not stop shining
until once again
the pool
turned into
a puddle.

And in the middle
of the puddle
sat two friends.
A frog named Fred
and a turtle named Ted.